HENRY HECKELBECK

Dinosaur Hunter

By **Wanda Coven**

Illustrated by **Priscilla Burris**

LITTLE SIMON

New York London Toronto Sydney New Delhi

LITTLE SIMON
An imprint of Simon & Schuster Children's Publishing Division
1230 Avenue of the Americas, New York, New York 10020
First Little Simon hardcover edition June 2021
Copyright © 2021 by Simon & Schuster, Inc.
Also available in a Little Simon paperback edition.
All rights reserved, including the right of reproduction in whole or in part in any form. LITTLE SIMON is a registered trademark of Simon & Schuster, Inc., and associated colophon is a trademark of Simon & Schuster, Inc.
For information about special discounts for bulk purchases, please contact Simon & Schuster Special Sales at 1-866-506-1949 or business@simonandschuster.com. The Simon & Schuster Speakers Bureau can bring authors to your live event. For more information or to book an event contact the Simon & Schuster Speakers Bureau at 1-866-248-3049 or visit our website at www.simonspeakers.com.
Designed by Leslie Mechanic
Manufactured in the United States of America 0521 FFG
10 9 8 7 6 5 4 3 2 1
Library of Congress Cataloging-in-Publication Data
Names: Coven, Wanda, author. | Burris, Priscilla, illustrator.
Title: Henry Heckelbeck, dinosaur hunter / by Wanda Coven ; illustrated by Priscilla Burris.
Description: New York : Little Simon, [2021] | Series: Henry Heckelbeck ; #6 | Summary: On a class field trip, Henry hopes to dig up a dinosaur bone with his lucky shovel.
Identifiers: LCCN 2021007773 (print) | LCCN 2021007774 (ebook) | ISBN 9781534486331 (paperback) | ISBN 9781534486348 (hardcover) | ISBN 9781534486355 (ebook)
Subjects: CYAC: Dinosaurs—Fiction. | Antiquities—Fiction. | School field trips—Fiction.
Classification: LCC PZ7.C83393 Hp 2021(print) | LCC PZ7.C83393 (ebook) | DDC [Fic]—dc23
LC record available at https://lccn.loc.gov/2021007773
LC ebook record available at https://lccn.loc.gov/2021007774

CONTENTS

Chapter 1 THE BIG DIG 1

Chapter 2 DREAM-A-SAURUS 19

Chapter 3 WISHBONE 31

Chapter 4 DIG THIS! 43

Chapter 5 FUNNY BONE 51

Chapter 6 BUTTONS AND BEANS 63

Chapter 7 FINDERS KEEPERS! 73

Chapter 8 T. REX-CeLLENT 85

Chapter 9 SKELETON CREW 97

Chapter 10 DINO-MITE! 107

Chapter 1

THE BIG DIG

Clump!

Clump!

Clump!

Henry opened and closed the cabinet doors in the family room.

"What are you looking for?" asked Mom.

Henry opened another door and said, "I'm looking for my FAVORITE shovel."

Mom raised an eyebrow.
Henry had a lot of favorite
things. He had a favorite
magnifying glass. He had a

Mom raised an eyebrow.
Henry had a lot of favorite
things. He had a favorite
magnifying glass. He had a

favorite soccer ball. He even
had favorite pirate coins. But
Mom had never heard of a
favorite shovel.

Henry's older sister, Heidi, hadn't heard of it either.

"You have a FAVORITE shovel?" she asked with a huff.

Henry sighed. "Well, of course I do! Doesn't EVERY kid have a favorite shovel?"

Heidi snorted. "I definitely DO NOT have a favorite shovel. And why do you need a shovel, anyway?"

Henry threw his hands in the air. "Um, for DIGGING! Why else would I need a shovel?"

Dad walked into the room and asked a very important question. "So, what are you going to dig?"

Henry hopped around and cheered, "Dinosaur bones!"

Dad nodded thoughtfully.

"And where are you going to find dinosaur bones in Brewster?"

"My class is going on a field trip to dig where the old bank building used to be," Henry explained.

"I didn't know dinosaurs used BANKS!" his sister said with a laugh.

Mom giggled too. "Was it the First Prehistoric Bank?"

Henry frowned. "Not funn[
need my favorite shovel i[
going to find anything [

Dad nudged Henry's arm. "Actually, I've heard some cool stuff from Brewster's past has been uncovered at the old bank."

Henry hung his head and mumbled, "Yeah, but no dinosaur bones."

This time nobody made a joke.

"So, what does your favorite shovel look like?" asked Mom, changing the subject.

Henry lifted his head a little.
"It has a wooden handle and
a steel scoop."

Mom's face lit up, and she stepped outside to pull something from the garden.

Then she came back into the house and held up her spade.

"Could *this* be your favorite shovel?" she asked.

Henry held out both hands. "That's it!"

Mom handed it to Henry. "Mystery solved!" she said. "Now go find those dinosaurs."

Chapter 2

DREAM-A-SAURUS

Henry flipped through his *Big Book of Dinosaurs.*

If I found a dinosaur bone, I would be the coolest kid in school, Henry thought. *Or the coolest kid in THE WORLD!*

Henry began to daydream about what it would be like to find a dinosaur bone.

He imagined tramping over dusty red rocks with a pail in one hand and a field kit on his back. It would be a perfect day for a dinosaur hunt.

"I think I spy something sticking out of that rock wall!" he would say.

Then he would hold a magnifying glass over his find. Could it be? It looked like the bone of a Tyrannosaurus rex, but bigger!

He would free the bone with a steel pick.

The Henry Heckelbeck-a-saurus

Henry wondered what it would be like to hold a real dinosaur bone in his hands. Or what it would be like to discover a new kind of dinosaur.

He would call it the Henry Heckelbeck-a-saurus!

Henry pictured himself at the Brewster History Museum next. He would cut the ribbon to the Henry Heckelbeck-a-saurus Exhibit, and the crowd would roar.

But that was just a dream.

As Henry doodled in his notebook, he didn't hear his sister walk into the room.

"What are you drawing?"
Heidi asked.

Henry covered his drawing with his arm. Heidi peeked over his shoulder and saw a sketch of a dinosaur skeleton.

"Okay, Henry," said Heidi. "If you DO dig up a dinosaur bone, which you never will, I promise to dress up like a dinosaur and hand out cookies at your exhibit."

Henry laughed. "That would be almost as cool as finding a dinosaur bone!"

Heidi rolled her eyes. "Whatever. I came to tell you dinner's ready," she said as she walked out of the room.

Henry looked back at his drawing. *Maybe I WILL dig up a dinosaur bone!* he thought. *Then my favorite shovel will become my LUCKY shovel!*

He laid his shovel on top of his doodles and headed downstairs.

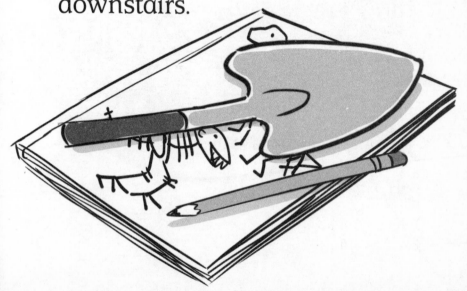

Chapter 3

WISHBONE

Henry sat up in bed in the middle of the night. A bright light shone in his room. *Is that the moon?* he wondered. He squinted at the glowing light.

No, that's not the moon!
That's my magic BOOK!

There had been an old book
on Henry's shelf since he was
a baby.

He didn't know it was magic until much later. But the book had always been by his side. It came to him in times of need.

Now the magic book was
floating to Henry along with
a medallion. The chain circled
Henry's head and came to rest
around his neck.

The book landed on his lap
and opened all by itself. Pages
began to flutter until they
stopped on a spell called the
Wishing Spell.

The Wishing Spell

What is your greatest wish?
Do you wish you had a puppy?
Or a swimming pool? Or perhaps
you wish to find treasure?
If your wish is pure and good,
then this is the spell for you!

Ingredients:
1 shovel
4 drops of glue
1 picture of what you wish for
1 wish filled with hope

Gather the ingredients in a mixing bowl. Then hold your medallion in one hand and place your other hand over the mix. Chant the following spell:

Diggery duggery dee!
Diggery duggery doo!
Give me a sign of a

_____.

(something you hope to find)

Then make my wish come true!

Henry gathered all the
ingredients, including a picture
of a dinosaur skeleton. Then
he wrote down his wish:

I WISH to
find a dinosaur bone.

Henry dropped his wish into the mix. Then he grabbed his medallion and chanted the spell.

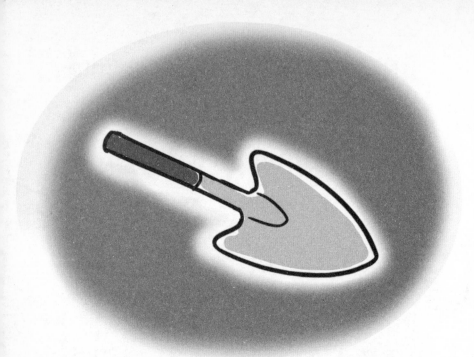

All of a sudden his shovel began to glow. Then a bright light flashed.

When Henry opened his eyes, his alarm was beeping.

His shovel no longer glowed,
the medallion was gone, and
the old book was back on his
shelf.

That's weird, Henry thought.
I must have been dreaming!

Chapter 4

DIG THIS!

On the day of the class dig, Henry brought his favorite shovel to school. It still hadn't glowed since the night before, but he kept checking—just in case.

"Why do you keep checking your backpack?" Dudley Day asked on the way to the dig site.

Dudley was Henry's best friend. They both liked to play spies and soccer.

Henry closed his backpack. "I don't want my books to crush my lucky shovel. That's all."

Dudley nodded as if he understood. "Hey, I brought my lucky shovel too!"

He pulled out a yellow beach shovel and showed it to Henry.

"Yeah, I built a blue-ribbon sandcastle with this!" Dudley said. "I got my picture in the newspaper and everything!"

Then somebody leaned over the boys' seat from behind. It was Max Maplethorpe. Max was the new girl. She was also a gifted spy and sometimes a little bit nosy.

"Check this out!" she said.
Max dangled her shovel in
front of the boys. It had a
built-in compass. Then she
pulled out a smaller shovel
from *inside* the handle.

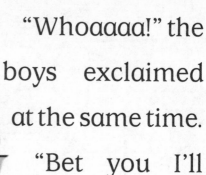

"Whoaaaa!" the boys exclaimed at the same time. "Bet you I'll find something REALLY special with THIS!" Max said as she slid the mini shovel back inside the handle.

Henry had no doubt she would find something special with a cool shovel like that.

What he did doubt was his own shovel. For one thing, his shovel didn't have any fancy hidden compartments. For another, it had never won a sandcastle contest.

And, worst of all, his shovel didn't even glow anymore. And maybe it never had.

Chapter 5

FUNNY BONE

The dig site was located in between a parking lot and a sandwich shop. Cars drove by it like it was nothing special. Plus, it was much smaller than Henry had expected.

A dinosaur skeleton would never fit here, he thought. *Unless it was a mouse-size dinosaur.*

Then his teacher, Ms. Mizzle, clapped her hands and said, "Class, I want you to meet Ms. Yards. She is a scientist, and she is going to tell us the history of this site."

Ms. Yards wore a large floppy green sun hat and scruffy hiking boots. She held a clipboard in her hand.

"Welcome, boys and girls!" she said. "Raise your hand if you know what used to be here."

Everybody's hands shot up. "A BANK!" they cried.

Ms. Yards nodded. "That's right! And before the bank, there was a grocery store here. And before the grocery store, there was a dressmaker's shop. And *way* before that, a home stood on this land."

Dudley raised his hand. "How do you know all that?"

"Good question!" Ms. Yards said. "One way we know is from town records. Another way we know is by the artifacts found on this site."

Now Ms. Mizzle raised her hand. Henry had never seen a teacher do that before!

"Can you explain what an artifact is?" she asked.

"Sure." Ms. Yards smiled as she held up an old chipped teacup.

"An artifact is something from the past that you *find* on a dig—like this teacup. Do you want to see more?"

The class followed Ms. Yards to a table covered with artifacts. There were coins, plates, buttons— even a rusty toy truck.

"We need your help to find more artifacts," said Ms. Yards.

Then Ms. Yards asked if the
kids had any more questions.

"Have you found any
DINOSAUR bones?" Henry
asked.

Everyone laughed except Ms. Yards.

"Not *yet*," she said, winking. "But maybe one of *you* will be the first!"

And nobody laughed at that.

Chapter 6

BUTTONS AND BEANS

Ms. Yards handed out paintbrushes, shovels, and buckets.

"What are the paintbrushes for?" Dudley whispered to Henry.

"To dust off your artifacts without hurting them," said Henry.

He showed his friend how to pick up a rock and dust off the dirt with his paintbrush.

Next the boys picked an area to dig. Dudley found something right away.

"It's a brass button that still has thread in the holes!" he cried.

Dudley ran to the tent to share his find. Henry went back to digging.

Then Max found something. "An arrowhead!" she cried.

Henry ran over and asked, "May I see?"

Max held it up for Henry to study.

"Sorry, Max," he said. "This isn't an arrowhead. It's just a really cool rock."

Max looked at her find more closely too.

"Huh, I guess you're right," she said. "But I'm STILL going to find something amazing!"

A few minutes later Max dug up an old pillbox.

Soon everyone began to find
stuff. They unearthed a ruler, a
lantern, a pair of suspenders,
and even an unopened can of
beans.

Henry was the only one who hadn't found anything.

"I thought this field trip was going to be fun," he complained under his breath.

Then he jammed his shovel into the ground. Only this time, when he pulled his shovel back out, it began to glow.

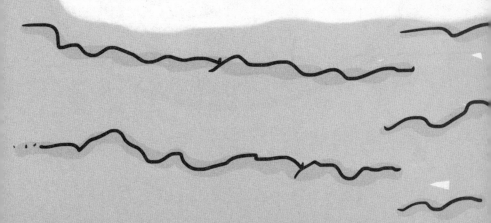

Chapter 7

FINDERS KEEPERS!

Henry stared at the glowing shovel and wondered what to do. But he didn't have to wait long. The shovel tugged his hand like a dog pulling on its leash.

73

The shovel dragged Henry to a corner of the site, where it plunged into the dirt.

"That's not a good place to dig!" called Ms. Yards. "We've already checked that area, and it's empty!"

Henry yanked his shovel out of the ground and stood up. But the shovel had a different idea. It pulled Henry right back down and began to dig all by itself.

Henry had to make it look like *he* was digging. What would his classmates think if they found out he had a *magic* shovel?

"Five more
minutes, Henry!"
called Ms. Mizzle.
Henry and
the shovel kept
digging.
"Okay!" he answered.

Now the shovel began to dig faster, like it knew it was running out of time.

Dirt flew everywhere.

Then—*CLICK!*—the shovel hit something.

Henry's heart began to beat faster as he dug around the object.

He pushed the shovel under the object and loosened it. Then he pulled it out of the ground.

"I FOUND something BIG!" Henry yelled, brushing the dirt off the object.

He waved his find in the air. Everybody came running.

"What is it?" asked Ms. Yards.

Henry couldn't believe what he held in his hands. "I think it's a DINOSAUR BONE!"

Chapter 8

T. REX-CELLENT

And Henry *had* found a dinosaur bone. His class crowded around him.

"May I touch it?" asked Dudley.

"Can I see?" Max asked.

"Are you going to name it?" asked somebody else.

Ms. Mizzle whistled. The class stopped talking.

"Henry has made an exciting discovery!" she said. "And now Ms. Yards will invite some other scientists to the site to look at it. We'll learn more after lunch."

Henry didn't want to leave his dinosaur bone, but knew he would see it again. His class had lunch at a park across the street. Henry, Dudley, and Max sat at a picnic table.

"That's silly, Max!" he said. "Whoever heard of a MAGIC shovel?!"

Max stopped laughing and raised an eyebrow. "I didn't say 'MAGIC' shovel, Henry. I said 'LUCKY' shovel. Are you hiding something?"

"You know what this MEANS?" asked Dudley, pulling a sandwich from his lunch bag. "It means you're going to be FAMOUS!"

Henry pictured his name in lights.

He didn't even notice when his magic shovel fell on the ground. Max picked it up.

"Henry! Be more careful!" Max scolded. "This shovel is VERY lucky. It was almost as if it did all the work FOR you!"

Henry sprayed a mouthful of milk on the table. Max and Dudley looked at each other and erupted in laughter. Henry wiped his face.

Henry kept up the fake laughter. "That's a good one, Max!"

He didn't want Max to get any more curious about his magic.

She was a spy, after all.

Ms. Yards was waiting for them when they got back to the site.

"Everyone, gather around!" she said excitedly. "We've now learned that Henry's bone is from a very *special* Tyrannosaurus rex! Is there anyone here who would like to help us dig for *more* dinosaur bones?"

Everybody's hands shot up.

"YES!" shouted the class.

And, of course, Henry yelled

the loudest.

Chapter 9

SKELETON CREW

Each scientist was paired with two students. Henry got to work with Ms. Yards.

Soon the class began to find more dinosaur bones. Henry unearthed the dinosaur's skull.

It was *so* cool, but not as big as Henry had imagined.

Dudley pulled a dinosaur hip bone from the dirt.

"I   found   a
HIP!" he cried.

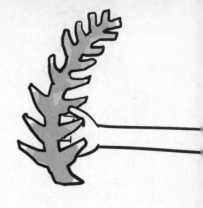

Other students
began to shout
about their finds
too.

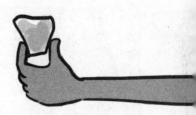

"I found a TAIL
bone!"

"I found a TOE
bone!"

"I found the
SPINE!"

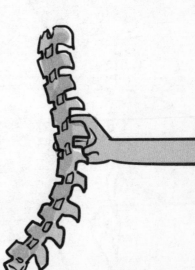

After two hours of digging, there were no more bones to be found. Everyone laid the bones on the tables.

"Since Henry discovered the dinosaur, he will help the scientists piece it together," said Ms. Yards.

The class cheered for Henry. He had never felt so important.

Then they began to assemble the dinosaur bones.

The bones snapped together easily, like plastic building blocks.

Putting this dinosaur back together is much easier than I expected! Henry thought.

Henry and the scientists worked quickly.

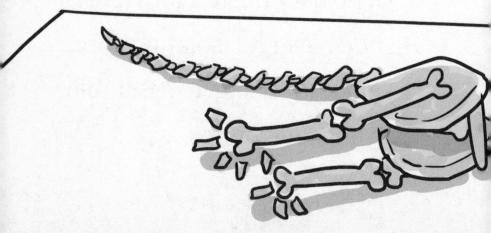

When the dinosaur was finished, it had a long tail, sturdy leg bones, and a skull full of razor-sharp teeth. The dinosaur wasn't nearly as big as Henry had expected.

"That's because it's from the *Grocery Period*," Ms. Yards told him.

Henry had never heard of the Grocery Period. But it didn't matter, because everybody *loved* his dinosaur—even the local TV news, who sent a reporter to the scene.

When the reporter asked
Henry how he had found
it, Henry held up his magic
shovel.

"I found it with this very
lucky shovel!" he said.

Chapter 10

DINO-MITE!

Henry had become a local star in Brewster. And today was the opening of his dinosaur exhibit at the Brewster History Museum. The crowd waiting outside was huge!

It was so big that Henry and Dad had to come in through the back entrance.

The dinosaur stood behind a large red curtain.

Ms. Yards waved Henry over.

"When I say your name, come stand on the stage beside me," she told him.

Henry nodded.

Then Ms. Yards stepped up to the microphone.

"Hello, everyone!" she said. "Today we truly have a one-of-a-kind exhibit to share. This discovery was made by one of our very own citizens, Mr. Henry Heckelbeck."

The crowd cheered as Henry walked onto the stage. Luckily, he had practiced exactly what he was going to say.

"I'm Henry," he began. "And I've named my discovery the Heckelbeck-a-saurus. And now I will reveal my one-of-a-kind dinosaur!"

Henry tugged a golden rope
that pulled back the red curtain
and revealed the skeleton. But
now the dinosaur held a sign
that read:

The crowd clapped and cheered. When everyone in the room quieted down, Ms. Yards explained that Henry's dinosaur once stood in front of the Brewster Grocery Store over fifty years ago.

"And without Henry," she added, "we may never have found the world's most fabulous *fake* dinosaur!"

Everyone congratulated Henry afterward. He even had his photo taken for the town newspaper.

But what Henry would never forget about that day was waiting for him at the refreshments table.

It was his sister, Heidi, dressed in a dinosaur costume and handing out cookies.

"NO WAY!" Henry exclaimed.
Heidi roared like a dinosaur.
"A promise is a promise!" she
said.

"But it wasn't even a REAL dinosaur!" Henry laughed.

Heidi shrugged. "But still, you discovered a DINOSAUR. That's pretty amazing."

Henry beamed at Heidi's kind words. "You know what?" he said. "You're a DINO-mite sister!"

Heidi held up her hands like a T. rex and roared. Then she said, "Well, only a dino-mite sister could have a bro-a-saurus like you!"

Henry Heckelbeck spied a new mystery behind the playground swing set.

"What's THAT?" he asked.

His best friend, Dudley Day, zoomed in on the object.

An excerpt from *Henry Heckelbeck Spy vs. Spy*

"My spy sense tells me it's personal property," he said.

The boys crept closer.

Henry smiled. "Well, my spy sense tells me its somebody's LUNCH BOX!"

Dudley put a finger to his lips. "Shh, not so loud. Remember Spy Rule Number Five!"

Henry covered his mouth with his hand. "Oops, sorry!" he whispered. "Spy Rule

An excerpt from *Henry Heckelbeck Spy vs. Spy*